Desert Critter Friends

THORNY TREASURES

Mona Gansberg Hodgson

Mona Gansberg Hodgson
Illustrated by Chris Sharp

Dad *Mssbaym*

CPH.
SAINT LOUIS

*Dedicated with much love and thanks to
Bob, my treasured husband and friend, and
with grateful love to Shirley, another dear
friend I treasure.*

*Special thanks to Susan Titus Osborn and
Nancy Sanders for sharing their editing skills
with me.*

Desert Critter Friends Series

Friendly Differences

Thorny Treasures

Scripture quotations taken from the HOLY BIBLE, NEW INTERNATIONAL VERSION®.
NIV®. Copyright © 1973, 1978, 1984 by International Bible Society. Used by
permission of Zondervan Publishing House. All rights reserved.
Copyright © 1998 Mona Gansberg Hodgson
Published by Concordia Publishing House
3558 S. Jefferson Avenue, St. Louis, MO 63118-3968
Manufactured in the United States of America

Library of Congress Cataloging-in-Publication Data
Hodgson, Mona Gansberg, 1954–
    Thorny treasures / Mona Gansberg Hodgson.
        p.   cm. — (Desert critter friends ; bk. 2)
    Summary: His desert animal friends save Lenny the pack rat from a
thorny predicament involving a hot air balloon, convincing him that
friends are the most important treasures. Additional text discusses how
Jesus is a person's best friend and the best treasure.
    [1. Wood rats—Fiction. 2.Desert animals—Fiction. 3. Hot air balloons—
Fiction. 4. Friendship—Fiction. 5. Christian life—Fiction.]
    I. Title. II. Series.
PZ7.H6649Th   1998
[E]—dc21   97-25811

1 2 3 4 5 6 7 8 9 10   07 06 05 04 03 02 01 00 99 98

Lenny, the pack rat, polished a purple bead with a leaf. Suddenly a noise outside his home surprised him.

Lenny dropped the bead on his pile of treasures. He kicked leaves, twigs, and pieces of cactus to hide his coins, buttons, and beads. Then he scurried to the door at the end of his log house.

"Hey, Lenny! You in there?" a voice called.

Lenny knew that voice. He poked his head out of the log. His large brown eyes looked out over the desert. Lenny saw Bert, the roadrunner. Bert paced back and forth.

"I'm here, Bert," Lenny answered.

"Super!" said Bert, racing up to the pack rat. "I'm going to explore down by the Verde River. It's the kind of day you like, friend—cloudy and cool. Want to come?"

Lenny raised
his whiskered nose in the air. He
looked up at the gray sky. Bert was
right. He did like this kind of
weather. But he didn't like to share.
If he went exploring with the
roadrunner, he might have to share
anything he found. What if he
found a really special treasure?

"Well?" Bert asked. "Are you coming? We could have fun together."

Lenny scratched his white throat. "Not today, Bert," he said. "I have too much to do."

"Okay." Bert sighed and took off across the desert. *Zoom!*

Lenny scurried back inside the log. He picked the cactus, twigs, and leaves off of his treasure pile. His furry brown body shook with delight. He looked at his bright treasures. They were all his! He held a shiny dime. Then he picked up a gleaming gold chain. *"Ooh!"*

Next Lenny rubbed a smooth red button against his nose. He thought about his treasures. The beads were round. The coins and the chain were shiny. The buttons were smooth. But he didn't have anything soft! And he wouldn't mind having more things that were round and shiny and smooth.

Suddenly Lenny got an idea. He would go on a treasure hunt!

Lenny put each piece of his
treasure in a hole in the floor of his
log home. In went the purple bead.
In went the shiny dime. In went the
gleaming gold chain.

Lenny piled twigs, leaves, and
cactus pieces on top of his
treasures. Then he tied on his fanny
pack and scurried outside.

11

Lenny wandered around rocks and under bushes. He traveled over a hill. Suddenly Lenny heard a rustling noise.

Lenny looked up. "*Wow!*" he squeaked. A big bouncing yellow balloon bobbed in the breeze above him. "*Ooh!*" His silky whiskers twitched with delight. There was more!

Shiny blue ribbons waved in the wind. The ribbons were tied to a basket stuck in a tree. What great treasures! Lenny didn't have a balloon or ribbons or a basket at home. He had found something big. Something colorful. And something soft!

Lenny looked to the left. He looked to the right. No one was in sight.

Lenny was glad Bert wasn't around. He wouldn't have to share. This best-ever treasure was all his!

Lenny scurried up the trunk of the acacia tree and out on a branch. "*Ouch!*" the pack rat yelled. He licked his paw where a thorn had stuck him. This wasn't going to be easy. But he wanted that thorny treasure!

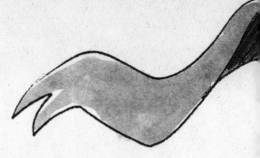

Lenny pulled on the basket.
Puff! Puff! The basket was stuck on
big thorns. *Tug! Tug!* He pulled
harder!

Plop! Lenny tumbled into the
basket. Where were the treasures?
Where were the shiny dimes?
Where were the round beads?
Where were the smooth buttons?
There was *nothing.* Nothing in the
basket.

Lenny's stomach did a
somersault. *Ugh!* What was
happening? He peeked over the top
of the basket. *Oh no!* He was
floating!

Lenny opened his eyes again and looked down at the desert. Where would the basket take him? How would he get back home? What would he do?

The pack rat wished Bert were there. Lenny sighed. He should have gone exploring with his friend. "Help! Help!" he squeaked. "Bert! Help, Bert!"

Just then the basket bounced and stopped. Lenny lost his balance again. *Plop!* Slowly he stood back

up on his back legs. He wasn't
floating anymore! He looked up
and saw leaves dancing in the
breeze.

Ach

Lenny peeked over the edge of the basket. He was stuck in a cottonwood tree. "Help me!" he cried. "Help!"

"*Achoo!*" Someone sneezed. Lenny's ears stiffened as he listened. "*Achoo!*" Another sneeze. Someone was on the ground below the tree!

"Help me!" Lenny shouted. "Help! Help!"

"Is someone up there?" a soft voice asked.

"Me!" Lenny answered. He looked down through the branches and saw a striped skunk staring up at him. "Rosie!"

"*Achoo! Achoo!* My allergies are terrible today." The skunk sniffed. "It's these desert weeds." Rosie frowned up through the leaves. "Lenny? How did you get up *there*?"

"I fell in the basket. It floated up. And now I'm stuck." The pack rat sighed. "Can you help me?"

"I bet you were looking for treasure," Rosie said. "You always are, you know."

"Yes, I was," Lenny whispered. He spoke in a louder voice. "Can you help me? I don't like flying—or sitting—in a basket."

"*Achoo!* Well …" The skunk giggled. "Maybe I could sneeze the ribbons loose, but I can't climb up there."

"This is no time for jokes!" Lenny answered. "I wish Bert were here. He'd know what to do."

"Why didn't you say so?" Rosie started to leave.

"Where are you going?"
Lenny asked.

"Don't worry. I'll come back.
Sniff! I saw Bert down by the water.
I'll go see if I can find him."

Lenny looked up at the cloudy
sky. What if Rosie didn't find Bert!
What would he do? He had his
treasures. But he had no friends.
Friends were more valuable than
any treasure—no matter how big or
colorful or soft.

A few minutes later Lenny heard Bert's voice.

"Hey! Lenny! You up there?"

"I'm here!" Lenny called. He peeked down at the roadrunner. "I thought you'd never get here!"

"I thought you were too busy to explore!" Bert said. "How did you get in this mess, anyway?"

"*Achoo!*" Rosie was back. "Lenny fell in the basket. It floated up, and now he's stuck," the skunk reported. "Can you get him down? *Sniff!*"

"We'll try," Bert said. The roadrunner paced under the tree. Back and forth. Back and forth. Back and forth. *Think! Think! Think!*

"You're making me dizzy!" Lenny said.

Bert stopped. "I have an idea!"
The roadrunner started
gathering sticks. "I will make
a ladder out of sticks. You can
climb up and grab the
basket," he told Rosie.

The skunk looked up at
Lenny. "It would have to be a
tall ladder. *Achoo!*"

"Never mind." Bert
said. "You'd sneeze. The
ladder would break, and
you'd fall." He paced some
more. *Think! Think! Think!*

"I know!" the skunk shouted.
Bert stopped pacing. Rosie said,
"We'll throw rocks at the balloon
and put a hole in it so it won't go
up. And we'll throw more rocks to
knock the ribbons off the branch.
Then the basket will come down."

"It sure will come down!"
Lenny shouted. "And I'll fall out
and land on my head!"

"*Achoo!*" Rosie sneezed.

"You have any better ideas?"
Bert asked Lenny.

"I do!" Lenny said. "Bert,
you're a bird! Why don't you fly up
here, free the ribbons, and carry the
basket down in your beak?"

"That's a great idea!" Rosie
said. "Why didn't I think of that?
Sniff!"

Bert paced in front of the tree. Back and forth. Back and forth. Back and forth. Then he stopped and cleared his throat. "I am a bird," he answered. "But I'm a roadrunner, not a skyflyer."

"But you have wings and feathers," Lenny argued. "You can fly, can't you?"

"*Achoo!* Can you fly, Bert?" Rosie asked.

"He's way up high," Bert told Rosie. "When I fly, it's usually for a short way—like up to a rock."

"Bert, please try," Lenny squeaked.

Bert looked up at Lenny. "I will try, but I still don't know if I can fly that high."

Bert rubbed his head with his wing. He wiggled out of his backpack. Then he spread his wings.

Lenny squeaked with excitement. Rosie clapped her fuzzy paws.

Bert flapped his wings and lifted himself into the air.

"Yes!" Lenny and Rosie both shouted.

Flutter! Flutter! Flutter! Bert tipped to the left. He tipped to the right. Then he landed on a nearby acacia tree.

"Sorry, Lenny," the roadrunner panted. He folded his wings. "I just don't think I can fly that high."

Just then the sound of thunder
roared over their heads. *Boom!*

"Oh, no," Lenny cried. "What if it starts to rain? The ribbons will come loose … and I can't fly!"

"Oh, no! *Sniff!*"

"I'll try again," Bert said. *Flap! Flap! Flap!* He went up. He tipped upside down.

"Oh, no!" cried Lenny.

"*Achoo!*" sneezed Rosie.

Flap! Flap! Flap! Bert straightened himself out. *Up, up, up* he went.

"You're doing it!" Rosie cheered.

Bert landed on a low branch of
the cottonwood tree. *Pant! Pant!* The
roadrunner was out of breath, but
he had made it.

"Yes!" Lenny and Rosie both shouted.

Bert hopped up to the branches where the ribbons were caught. *Up, up, up* he hopped. "Hi, Lenny. You ready to get down yet?"

"Very funny, Bert!" the pack rat squeaked.

"Hang on!" Bert grabbed the ribbons with his beak. Lenny did a somersault as Bert's wings whipped the wind.

Lenny tipped to the left. Then he tipped to the right. Then he felt a bump! *Plunk!* He was safely on the ground.

Lenny crawled out of the basket. He held the rim with his paws to keep it from flying away.

"I'm so glad you're safe," Rosie said. *"Sniff!"*

"Thanks for finding Bert so he could help me." Lenny saw the roadrunner resting under a tree.

Lenny looked at the balloon. His friend was more important than even this special treasure. The pack rat grabbed a ribbon in his mouth. He dragged the basket over to the roadrunner. "I want you to have this, Bert," he said. *"Puff! Puff!"*

"But Lenny, you got in all that trouble to get your thorny treasure," Bert said.

"I know, but I want you to have it," answered the pack rat. "You are a good friend."

"*Achoo!*"

Lenny turned toward the skunk. "You too, Rosie. I found out today that friends are the most important treasures."

"Let's drag the basket back to your place, Lenny," Bert said. "We can set it up outside."

"We can have a party," Rosie said. "All your friends will see that bright yellow balloon bobbing in the breeze."

"I will put my treasures inside the basket," Lenny squealed. "And to show my friends that *they* are treasures, I will give a button, a bead, or a coin to each one when they come for the party!"

Jesus is your very best friend. And He is your treasure too! He loves you so much that He gave His life for you. He will help you share that love with your friends.

For where your treasure is, there your heart will be also. Matthew 6:21

Hi, kids!

God's Word tells us that Jesus is our best friend and our best treasure. The word search on the next page is full of words that tell us what good friends do. You can read about each word in the Bible verse listed next to it. Then find all the words in the basket.

forgive   **Luke 5:20**

guide   **Proverbs 27:9**

help   **Ecclesiastes 4:10 and Luke 11:8**

love   **Proverbs 17:17 and John 15:13**

pray   **3 John 1:2**

wait and **listen**   **John 3:29**

For Parents and Teachers:

Kids can't turn on the TV, ride to the store with you, or read a magazine without being bombarded by ads enticing them to want more things. From a particular brand of cereal to a cool new toy, advertisers know how to push emotional buttons to promote their products.

We all have to admit that we sometimes, like Lenny, give in to materialism. We allow our obsession with things—our quest for more—to interfere with relationships. Like Lenny, we are tempted to ignore or neglect our friends in pursuit of material gain.

God, through the work of His Holy Spirit, has placed our greatest treasure in our hearts—faith and love for Jesus, His Son and our Friend and Savior. Help your children see that our true treasure is not found in things, but in God's love. As we share His love with one another, we build solid friendships to treasure as well.

Here are some questions you can use as discussion starters to help your children understand these concepts.

Discussion Starters

1. What is Lenny doing in the beginning of the story?

2. Why does Lenny decide not to go exploring with Bert?

3. What did Lenny decide to do on his own? Do you think that was a good plan? Why or why not?

4. What did Lenny find out about treasures and friends while he was stuck in the basket?

5. Do you have friends like Bert and Rosie who help you? Tell how a friend has helped you.

6. Why is Jesus your very best friend and treasure?

7. What can you do to share Jesus' love with others?

Pray together. Thank God for your friends and your children's friends. Then thank Him for sending His Son to be your best friend and treasure.

Why is Jesus your very best friend and treasure? Tell me by writing on these lines.

_____

_____

_____

_____

_____